PRAISE FOR

TROY'S AMAZING UNIVERSE:

"The wisest people have written for children, this is certainly true of Sharon Kennedy Tosten's love letter to her son....This book will touch your heart... Very seldom has such a poignant subject been told with such love and compassion."
Kristen J. Johnson, MY SHELF.com

"Children are going to love it. It is full of fun, action and adventure, as well as an excellent message. Great job."
Margaret Chapman, Blether Book Reviews

"The fourth graders could not get enough of Troy and begged me every class to continue. It was wonderful to see the enthusiasm all the children showed for reading. I wish all their books would hold their interest as your book."
Linda Valenti, Saint Ignatius Loyola Grammar School Librarian

Troy's Amazing Universe
K For Karate

Sharon K. Tosten

Printed in the United States of America.
Edited by Yvonne Bonomo

Brite Press
2006

Troy's Amazing Universe
K For Karate

Sharon K. Tosten

Dedication

To all of the amazing Black Belts at Amerikick-
and especially to the Senior instructors, Dennis Tosten,
Mark Russo, Michael Sautner, Michael Semeriglia, Justin
Smith, Nick Dougherty, Nick Perdunn, Chris Millares,
Tim McCandless, Kevin Schlueter, Jason Helmer, Mike
Recinto, Alex Davydov and Mark Gallagher. Thanks for
your spirit and dedication. Special thanks to Jon and
Lauren Ellis for "The Dragon."

CHAPTER 1

Why did all the kids run away from my table?

"Hey everybody, watch this!" Allen said.

I smell something funny. I think that is Allen talking. I don't hear perfect, but I can tell who everyone is by the way they smell. Allen smells like trees, big trees. Allen has the most muscles in our school. He looks like a grown up, but he is only ten years old. That is different from me—I am the smallest kid in the whole school. My name is Troy. I am eating my apple for lunch. Everybody likes to talk at lunch. I just eat at lunch. Other kids at my table talk and eat, and read at the same time. I want to know how to do that. Allen's nose is kind of flat on his face and is the same color as one of my freckles. All of him is the same color as one of my freckles. Should I run away, too? Uh oh oh... My apple is rolling off the table.

"I am the strongest man in the world!" Allen said.

Allen is picking my school lunch table and bench up. I am going to fall off! Hold!

"SPLASH!"

My grape juice spilled on me. That is not good. My shirt is...was white. Everything inside me is hurting. My head feels like somebody is inside hitting me with a hammer. My stomach has rocks jumping around in it and my eyes are shaking. Why didn't my feet run away?

"HA! Ha...ha...ha... That is so funny. However, Mr. G will be coming back through that door in 2.4 seconds," laughed Wyatt.

Wyatt laughs loud. It sounds like a machine gun. He is real smart. Wyatt won the spelling bee and the math bee. There are no colors on Wyatt. His skin is white, his hair is white, and his teeth are big and white. From up here I can see everybody laughing and this is not funny. I can see all the way across the room. Chad, the tallest kid in school, is at the water fountain. He is so tall he has to bend way over to get a drink. He is pushing the button but no water is coming out. My hands are shaking. I was supposed to run like the other kids.

"Allen! Put Troy down!" yelled Mr. G.

OH NO! I'm falling!

CHAPTER 2

We are at the office. My Dad is here. His hair is red like mine. He smells like leather. Dad is sitting in front of Mr. G's desk, next to all of us. He does not look happy. Mr. G does not look happy either. His black eyebrows are scrunched. Mr. G has lots of hairs on his eyebrows, but zero hairs on his head.

"Ha! I was never in the office before!" said Wyatt.

Wyatt smells like water, the kind that comes out of the drink fountain.

"Me either," said Allen.

"Why did you pick up the lunch table Troy was sitting at, Allen?" Mr. G asked.

Allen is looking at the floor. "I don't know."

I know, because I didn't run. Everybody knew when it was time to run, but not me. Why am I last all of the time?

"Allen, you do know. Troy's father is here and wants to know why you would choose to chance injuring his son."

Allen crosses his feet. "I don't know."

Mr. G leaned over the desk and asked, "Allen, why would you pick on Troy? Did he do something to bother you? Maybe Troy should stay after school?"

This is not going good. I watch T.V. after school.

"Wyatt said I couldn't pick up a lunch table full of kids," Allen said.

Is that true, Wyatt?" asked Mr. G, crinkling his eyebrows a little more.

"Ha! Yes, and we still don't know if he could because the other three kids ran," laughed Wyatt.

"I could have!" Allen snapped at Wyatt.

"You're very lucky Troy didn't get hurt. You both should thank Chad," said Mr. G.

When Mr. G yelled in the lunch room, Allen turned around and I slid off the bench. Chad jumped over everyone and caught me. Chad's legs are real long like a giraffe has. He is the fastest runner I ever saw.

"You both have detention for a week," announced Mr. G.

NO! Now they will not be my friends. They will be mad at me because they got in trouble.

"Ha! Excuse me Mr. G, but technically I didn't *do* anything. Therefore I deserve no penalty," said Wyatt.

"You're very smart, Wyatt. Next time use your intelligence for good things. Go to detention."

Allen and Wyatt look mad at me. I got them in trouble.

"Let's go, Troy," said Dad.

I made my Dad sad. His eyes are red. I was supposed to run like everybody else.

"Mr. Tomler," said Mr. G.

That is my Dad's other name.

"Take this card. You might want to take your son to this place. The other boys go there. It will help him," said Mr. G.

"Those boys go there? It doesn't seem to be helping them," said Dad.

"It will. Go there now. They're expecting you," said Mr. G.

WHOA! What happened to Mr. G's face? It turned orange, now purple, and blue and his eyes, they pointed way up to the sides. His eyebrows- they are kind of moving. Dad! Don't you see it? Dad is just nodding. Dad! Look at his face! Uh oh oh, his face went back to regular.

"I'll take him there," said Dad.

Dad! Didn't you see his face? Dad is still nodding. Mr. G is giving Dad the little card. It has a dragon on it. The dragon is looking at me.

CHAPTER 3

"You alright, Troy? asked Dad.

Dad isn't saying anything about Mr. G's face. How come he didn't see it?

"Troy, are you alright? I'm talking to you," said Dad.

Oh. Nod yes. Sometimes I forget to answer, especially when I see peoples' faces turn orange and purple. We are walking to the mini van. At least I get to go home early from school today. I am not hurt, but my shirt is all purple from grape juice. I tried to clean it up in the bathroom, but the water wasn't coming out good, just drips. Tell Dad I am okay. "Okay." Uh oh oh! OOPS! I fell on a bump in the ground.

Lucky Mom didn't see that. If she saw me fall, we would have to get an ice pack or maybe an x-ray.

"Come on, Troy. Get up and get in the car," said Dad.

Oh. I was just taking a rest. Dad is looking at me very sad, like he doesn't know why I fall down. I don't know either.

"Try to pay attention, Troy. Don't look at the ground, look up."

I see clouds. That one looks like a gummie bear.

"Not up...I mean look at the road ahead. Look at what's right in front of you."

Dad is right in front of me. I will look at him. Hmmm. Here is a string on his shirt...pull it.

"Never mind, Troy..."

Dad is holding my hand now. Now in front of me is our mini van. It is green.

"Troy, I'm going to put you in a new sport," Dad said when we got into the car.

I don't want to do any more sports. Mom is looking for an activity for me. It is not going good. I went to some sports, but so far, none of them are working. I hit the ball in baseball, but I didn't run faster than the ball, so I never made it to a base. Soccer was very hard. You have to run and kick the ball at the same time and my feet got all tangled up. I fell down and it wasn't any fun. Dad said he would take me to football, but Mom won't let me try football. She said it's too dangerous and I could get crushed and end up in the hospital again. Water is scary, so that leaves out swimming and diving and everything else you get wet at. I am good at the little golf, but I can't hit the ball far to play the real kind.

"Oom-my?" What about Mom? She has rules about sports.

I have trouble saying some letters, but Dad sometimes knows what I am saying. I wish everyone could understand my words. I know he won't understand me trying to say 'Mr. G has a purple and blue face'.

"Mom had to take a nap...her headaches are bothering her," said Dad.

My mom has headaches sometimes, so Dad and I know it is not a good time to talk to her.

"So I'm not taking you home right now," said Dad.

I hope we're going to get chicken nuggets. Mom doesn't let me have drive thru dinner, but Dad always does.

"I am going to take you to try out this new sport." Are there any left?

"Don't worry, Troy. This will be fun. It's inside."

I hope it's not basketball again. Somehow the ball kept knocking me over. Last time my dad brought me there, the coach man gave him a funny look and let out a big breath, like Mom does when she walks in my room and stuff is all over the floor.

We are here. I know because the car is not moving anymore. There is a sign in the window of the place in front of us. K-A-R-A-T-E. I can't read except for some words, but I know my letters. Wyatt would know what that spells. I think that says 'carrot.' I hope not. I am not hungry for vegetables right now.

"Come on in, Troy. This is it. You are going to try a karate lesson."

I know Mom doesn't know about this.

"Troy, get out of the car. Mr. G said this will be good for you. It'll be fun."

I don't think my Dad knows what is fun. Being hit with a ball is not fun, and I don't think being hit with a foot will be fun at all. And I don't want to do anything Mr. Green face thinks is fun. Why can't he just get me a karate CD game? That is fun.

"Come on, I'm pretty sure that this is the same place Krista goes."

Krista is my cousin. She is three years older than me. She lives next door and she plays with me when her friends are not home. Krista is good at everything. Her feet run fast and jump high and she can turn upside down in the air without hitting her head. Krista doesn't fall down and she has never even been to the hospital except to get born.

"Are you getting out of the car?" asked Dad.

No. Nod my head no, no, no.

"Or do I have to drag you out?"

Oh. I thought the *no* was going to work that time.

"Come on."

I better go. He is going to drag me out. This works much better with my mom. She usually promises me a new Octane Octopus under water super hero game or something if I get out of the car nice. He grabbed me. WHOOSH! I am out of the car. I was going to come by myself soon. Dad has my hand—not too tight—but I don't think I will be able to escape.

"Now we'll go inside and the karate teacher is going to give you a private lesson...just you and him."

Uh oh oh, I will be the only one there for him to kick.

"He's a black belt," Dad smiled.

Why is Dad smiling? Krista has that game "BLACK BELT FIGHTER." The guys have arms so big that their shirts are all torn up, and long teeth and fingernails they scratch each other with, and they swing big chains and sticks. They fight in a castle with Dracula bats and fire and the walls fall down and...No!

"Troy, walk. We're going inside."

No. Nod no, no, no.

"Let's go."

Dad is looking strong at me with his eyes. I am going. I don't know why. My feet are just going. When is the fun?

This place is big—kind of a big white empty room with a red floor, and it smells a little bit like feet after they come out of an old sneaker. There are some chairs in the front and a little counter. A man is behind the counter. I don't see any Dracula bats.

"Hi, is this Troy?" asked the man.

"Yes. Say hi, Troy," Dad said pushing me forward. Wave.

"Hi, Troy. Nice to meet you."

The man is coming out from behind the counter. Uh oh oh. He is wearing a black belt.

"I'm Dennis. I'll be working with you today."

Dennis? That is not a black belt name. It is supposed to be like, 'Yakura, Chain Master.' He doesn't look like a black belt either. On his head is blond hair, and just regular teeth are in his mouth, and his shirt is not torn up at all. The beach—that is what he smells like, like the white stuff Mom rubs all over me when we are at the beach. My Mom smells like warm muffins. I wonder what the guys in "BLACK BELT FIGHTER" smell like? Ew. Dennis might smell better than them. I guess he probably doesn't kick as hard as the guys with the big giant arms. Good.

"Here's your uniform. Put it on and we'll get started," said Dennis.

My Dad is giving Dennis some money. You have to pay to get kicked?

"Okay, let's get started, Troy. Just step up on the mat. Uh oh oh! OOPS! I fell...forgot to step up. Hmm... This red mat thing is soft. Falling here will be better than at the other places.

"That's okay, just let me help you up and stand up straight," said Dennis.

This Dennis guy smiles nice. He doesn't growl at all like the guys in the game. His uniform has a dragon on it. Just like the card Principal G gave him! I am looking hard. The dragon's eyes are not moving.

"You can call me Sensei Dennis. Sensei is a Japanese word that means teacher."

"En ay En es." Sensei Dennis. Wow. I can say Japanese words as good as I say regular words.

"Now first we bow in. Put your hands together like this."

Uh oh oh. What did he do? That was too fast.

"Here, let me show you. Take this hand and squeeze it into a fist."

He is putting my hands the way they are supposed to go. I am glad no other kids are here. They sometimes do what the coach wants right away, and they all don't like to wait for me. Okay, he put my hands where they are supposed to go. I will stay like this. My hands always forget where they are supposed to go.

"Good job!"

I did it right? Wow.

"Okay, now let's try our first kick."

Kick? No! Go to Dad! Go. Go. Go. Dad! Hold Daddy's leg.

"Troy, what's wrong? Go back out and work with Sensei Dennis. Don't be a baby."

People don't kick babies.

Dad is trying to pull my hands off his leg. "Come on, Troy. Go back on the mat and try."

No. Hide my face. I want to go home. I don't want to get kicked. Now they are saying things. I am not hearing them. I want to go home.

"Come on, Troy," Dad said.

We're going home? Yes.

"You have to try."

No. I am not moving. No. I smell the beach smell. Sensei Dennis is patting me on the back. Not hard, though.

"Look, why don't you come back tomorrow and we'll try again? You can come and watch the other kids."

Watch? I can watch. That is something I am good at. Good. Now we are going home. Dad is pulling me out the door. I always walk too slow for him.

Two grown-up guys are coming in the karate door. Both of them have black hair on their heads and are holding black belts in their hands. One man has a nose that looks like the back of a camel. The other one is sort of bony and hunched, and his skin looks like the people who lay out in the sun all day with slippery stuff on them. Wait! What is that? On the back of the camel nose guy, a fin like on a shark is sticking out, and the bony guy has a tiger tail. Whoosh! They are gone.

CHAPTER 4

"Ron! Why is Troy wearing karate clothes?" Mom screeched.

Uh oh oh. Mom will not like this at all. A dish is in her hand and she is scrubbing it very hard. Not much water is coming out of the faucet, just a skinny line. Mom keeps wiggling it, but it doesn't help. Mom cleans all day long. I don't know where all the dirt is, because she even sweeps with the broom outside so we don't walk any dirt in.

"Troy tried out his first karate class. He did really well. Didn't you, Troy?"

I did? Thanks, Dad. Smile. I didn't tell Dad about the shark fin and the tiger guy. He wouldn't understand me anyway.

"What are you, crazy? Somebody could kick him. You want him to end up in the hospital again?" said Mom.

Good. Now I won't have to go back.

"It's perfectly safe."

"Dance is safe. Take him to dance."

"No," said Dad.

"What is wrong with dance?"

I never saw my dad dance. I don't even think you can dance to the music he listens to. When it's on the radio he plays a make-pretend guitar and shakes his head funny.

"Give this a chance. I think it will be good for him," Dad answered.

They just talk like I am not even here. I am taking off this uniform thing. Uh oh oh, it has a dragon on the back.

"What if he decides to hit the kids in school with it, then what?"

"They teach them not to do that. It's very safe. I'm taking him tomorrow. He has to do something besides sit around here."

"Fine, but if he gets hurt you can run him to the emergency ward this time!"

I think my mom and dad are going to have a discussion. I hope it is not a real loud one.

"He won't get hurt. Krista has been doing it for two years and she never got hurt."

"Krista is an athlete," Mom said.

What is an athlete? If Krista is one, I think I would like to be one.

"He won't get hurt...stop being ridiculous."

"Ridiculous? Fine, take him then and he'd better not get hurt."

Mom is going back upstairs. Wait! Where is Mommy going? She is letting Daddy take me back there?

Something is not the same with Mommy. When she says I can't go somewhere, I never get to go. Hmm...?

CHAPTER 5

"KIAAA!"

There are a bunch of kids here kicking and making a lot of sounds.

"Attention!"

Sensei Dennis is teaching all the kids. Most of them are bigger than me. Some are my size. Sensei Dennis is not kicking any of them. They are just kicking in the air. In "BLACK BELT FIGHTER" you get zero points if you kick the air. Dad is pushing me to the mat.

"You ready to get in, Troy? Your class is next."

Get in? Today is just watching. Watching. I thought this would happen. That is why he made me wear the karate clothes. Sit. I am not going. I am watching.

"Come on, Troy. Give it a try," said Dad.

No. Nod no. I am watching. I can't get hurt watching. Mommy will be mad if I get hurt.

"Troy! How come you are just sitting there? You are supposed to line up for class."

Krista! It is my cousin Krista! She smells like flowers. A belt is around her waist. It is red.

"Come on. Let me help you get in."

I will go in with Krista...she never kicks me.

Everybody is moving their hands very fast doing something Sensei Dennis is calling a "Wrap Around." They are grabbing each other, then the kid getting grabbed wraps his arm around and twists the other kid all up. Where are the animal guys? I don't see them anywhere. I want to know how they made the fin and tail disappear. This karate is too hard to do. Krista is making my hand move.

See, Troy? This is a chop block. Just bring your arm up and out. Good. Just like that. You use it if someone tries to punch or kick you. You just go 'chop block.' See? Then the punch won't hit you."

Maybe I should I learn this.

"Try again, Troy, and yell loud. "KIAA!""

"Ahh! Krista sounds like my aunt's cat when I stepped on his tail by mistake. Some of the other kids are laughing.

"A KIAA is supposed to come from your gut, not your nose, Krista," said Allen.

Uh oh oh... Why is he here? He looks bigger and scarier in karate clothes.

"Just ignore him, Troy," said Krista. "Try the block again."

Bring my arm up. I'm tired. Uh oh oh, now they are doing something else. Too fast. Sit down.

"Come on, Troy. You have to try."

I don't think I do.

"Troy, just try and I will get you gummies after class."

Gummies? I will stand up.

"Good. Now watch Sensei Dennis," said Krista.

Sensei Dennis is standing on one foot and holding his other foot up to his head. He is not falling over at all.

"Troy, now just lift your knee up."

Uh oh oh. BAM! I fell down. I don't like this.

"Get up, Troy, and try again. You can do it."

I can do it? Krista thinks I can do it? She is wrong. Oh, they are doing the bow thing. I can do that...it means it is over. Good. Bow.

"Good job, Troy. Give me high five."

Where are the gummies? Krista is holding up her hand. High five. I smell the beach smell, Sensei Dennis. Where are the animal guys?

"Great job today, Troy. I can't wait to see you in the next class."

Next class? I have to come back again? Dad is grabbing my hand. Aunt Nancy is here. She is Krista's mom. Dad is leaning to me.

"Troy, you can come to karate with Krista. I am going to drive you both here and Aunt Nancy is going to drive you both home. That way you can come to karate three times a week."

Three? I wanted zero times. Karate is not fun. Shake my head no.

"You can do this, Troy. You'll be good at it. It will be fun...you'll see...and Krista will help you. Won't you, Krista?"

"Sure, Troy. I'll help you."

"You want to do this with Krista, don't you, Troy?"

Aunt Nancy is patting my shoulder with her hand. She has red hair like me. I don't think they will let me go home until I say yes. Smile. Nod yes.

"Good. Let's go home, Troy," said Dad.

Yes, that worked. Maybe next time I will see the animal guys. I didn't get my gummies.

Mommy is upstairs. I think she is sick again—too sick to stop Daddy from taking me to karate.

CHAPTER 6

"Troy, turn around."

Huh? Oh, Sensei Dennis is telling me to turn a different way again. I am always facing the other way as everybody else. Maybe he wants us all to face the same way? Why? What is that smell? It smells like the dead worms from when Dad took me fishing, and I fell off the boat and Mom said no more water sports for me. I don't like water. The worms smell is coming from the shark fin guy! He's here! But there is no fin on his back. He is just walking around the mat looking at everyone. His mouth is like in a smile, but not his eyes. They are brown like mud and are real close to his camel nose. Where did he put the fin?

Krista is whispering in my ear. "That is Sensei Sal. I never saw him do any karate. He just walks around and looks mean at everybody."

Hmm...I would like to do that kind of karate.

"Bow."

Class is over. I have to watch now. Krista's mom is coming after Krista does a special karate team class. There are only four kids on the team. They have red, white and blue karate clothes, and the back says "A-M-E-R-I-K-I-C-K T-E-A-M." Chad with the giraffe legs from school is here. He is jump-kicking at a target real fast. OOPS! He missed it again. He is not happy.

"It's alright. Try to not be so nervous. Relax, and you'll hit it," said Sensei Dennis.

"I always miss," said Chad.

Wyatt is here and his skin is so white it looks like he never went outside ever. Wyatt's legs go way over his head. He can bend all different ways like Krista's Barbie dolls that I am not allowed to touch ever.

"Wyatt, that kick is high, but it needs more power," said Sensei Dennis. "Put some focus in it."

"Ha," said Wyatt.

Wyatt kicks real high, but he doesn't make the karate face like the other kids. His face just looks like he is watching T.V.

There is another girl, Monica, who has no freckles at all. I have them all over me. She is always jumping around like she is never tired, and her hair is so long I think she could sit on it. I don't know because she never sits down. She is swinging a stick and she keeps dropping it.

"Take your time, Monica...you're too wild! Look where you're spinning," said Sensei Dennis.

OOPS! She dropped it again. Sensei Dennis is helping everyone. No moms and dads are watching today—just me. Everybody here is good at karate. They

jump and spin and sit on the floor with their legs all the
way apart. I know that hurts, because I tried it. My legs
don't go all the way apart...they get stuck. Allen and his
big muscles are here. Allen looks like his legs are stuck,
too. He can't sit all the way down. "Allen, try turning
your toes this way. It will help you get your split lower,"
said Sensei Dennis.

"I can't do it that way. I'm just not flexible," said
Allen.

"Try it."

"It won't work," Allen replied.

Sensei Dennis shook his head. "You'll never have a
flexible body without a flexible mind."

Allen has just regular white karate clothes like me.

"Speaking of flexible minds, Sensei...can I be on the
team now?" asked Allen.

"No," said Sensei.

Allen looked at the floor. "I come to team practice
every week!"

"I told you not to," answered Sensei Dennis.

"Sensei, I've come to every practice for two years!
Doesn't that mean anything?"

"It means you're stubborn." Sensei Dennis is
bending toward Allen. "Allen, I like you...but for
international competitions...you're not cut out for it. You
need to have more natural abilities. It would hurt the
team."

Wow. That is not nice. Allen looks sad. That is
funny. Allen is not going home. He is going back on the
mat and practicing his kick. He does the same kick over
and over and over.

Worms. I smell them. Sensei Sal is next to me. "Why are you here? He won't let you on the team."

I feel cold. The air coming out of his mouth is like when I forget to close the freezer at my house and lots of white air comes out.

Sal is talking lower. "He never let me on and I'm great. Don't waste your time. You'll never be one of them."

Good. I do not want to be on a team. I am shaking. Just inside my hands...and my arms...and my legs...and my feet...and my head. My head is shaking a lot.

"KIII!" Krista yelled.

Sensei Dennis is making a funny face every time Krista yells.

"Krista, try to breathe from the bottom of your stomach. It will give you more power," said Sensei Dennis.

The worm smell went away. Sensei Sal is standing at the counter. There is the Tiger Tail guy! He is giving something to Sensei Sal—a little box. I can see the fin and the tail again. Get Krista. Point. Krista is not looking at me. Nobody is. The music is on and they are all practicing and looking in the mirror. Point to Sal. Look, Krista!

A discussion. Sensei Sal and Tiger Tail are having what my mom says is a discussion. They are making mean faces and pointing their hands at each other. It is not nice.

Whoosh! The Tiger Tail guy is gone. Uh oh oh, Sensei Sal is coming over here. His fin is shrinking into his back. His mud eyes, they see me. He is only a few steps away. It feels like cold water is washing on me. I never want to be on this team. Wow. Chad can jump up high. They all look like they are having a fun time. How come when somebody tells you to not do something, you want to do it? My mom tells me not to touch stuff in the store all of the time. Then I have to touch it. Sometimes it breaks. I don't want to be on the team. Yes I do.

The music stopped. Sensei Sal stopped walking over to here. Sensei Dennis is clapping his hands. "Everyone, over here. Wait here and Sensei Sal will give you our competition schedule. We're going to have a terrific, awesome season!"

Sensei Sal is going back to the counter and grabbing papers. He is making a not nice face at Sensei Dennis. Sal is coming back here. I am going far away. I will wait next to the door for Aunt Nancy.

Dennis is real smiley telling all the kids on the team good stuff like, "Monica, your kicks are really fast...and Krista, I've never seen you jump so high." Sal is giving out papers. He is not saying anything nice, just, "Pay attention. Here's your schedule."

Maybe Sal needs Dennis to say nice things to him, too. Allen is still doing his kick. Nobody is saying anything to Allen or to me.

I see the little box on the counter that Tiger Tail left here. It has lots of pictures on it. I like to look at pictures. Pick it up. On the front is a purple and red dragon with...

"Put that down!" Sensei Sal is running to me. OOPS! The box fell down. Cards with animal pictures are spilling all over the floor. Sal is screaming. "NOOO!"

The pictures are moving. WHOOSH! The karate doors are closing all by themselves. "THUMP! THUMP! THUMP!" Something black is melting over the windows. "SWISH!" WHOOSH! The roof just flew off! CRASH! CRASH! CRASH! CRASH! All the walls fell down! It is dark.

CHAPTER 7

"Nobody move," Sal said.

Someone is grabbing my hand. "I got you, Troy. Don't be scared." Krista. I am glad she is my cousin.

"Here are some gummies," said Krista.

I am very glad she is my cousin. Put the gummies in my pocket.

"Stop this, Sal!" Sensei Dennis screamed and fire flew out of his mouth.

Fire is coming out of Dennis's mouth! Wow! I can see. We are not in the karate school anymore. We are outside at night. It isn't like outside at my house. The trees are short and more wiggly. I don't see any houses...just trees and grass. I think I hear water. A big bluish moon is coming up in the sky. It is so big if I put up both hands in front of my face I can still see it, and the stars are bluish, too. That is funny. The rest of the sky is turning kind of grayish like the regular moon. It's all backwards.

"Roar!"

"What was that?" Monica asked.

It sounded like a big lion, not too close.

"ROAR."

Closer. Allen is standing up! "Shut up out there or I'm gonna come and get you! You're scaring the little girl."

"Ha! Go ahead and get him, Allen!" said Wyatt.

"ROAR! ROAR! ROAR!"

"Maybe not," Allen said and sat down.

"We have to deal the cards now, Dennis!" Sal yelled.

The other kids' mouths are being quiet, but they are screaming with their eyes. I think Krista's hand is shaking, but maybe it is mine.

"Put the cards back in the box!" Dennis screamed.

More fire is coming out of Dennis's mouth. Something is funny with his eyes. They are turning up at the ends.

"Splash!" Something is jumping in the water.

"What did you do? Take us home!" Krista is yelling at Sensei Sal.

"SPLASH!"

"I have to go! Dennis, deal the cards!" Sal is running away. "SPLASH!"

He jumped into the water.

"ROAR!"

Dennis is grabbing the box. The cards are moving around on the ground. "Don't touch the cards! I have to put them back," Dennis yelled.

"ROAR!"

"I have to go!" Chad is getting up and running away. Dennis is trying to grab up the cards, but they are moving fast around.

"Sensei, you have to get Chad!" Krista said grabbing Dennis.

"Someone get him! I have to get these cards!" Dennis yelled.

"HAAA! None of us can catch him. He's the fastest kid in the state!" Wyatt laughed.

"ROAR! THUMP. THUMP. THUMP!"

"It's chasing him! It's chasing him!" Monica said.

Monica is right...I can hear it. The roaring thing is chasing after Chad.

"Hold these!" Dennis shoved the cards into Allen's hands.

Dennis is chasing after Chad. I think Dennis is growing a tail. The cards are moving toward us.

CHAPTER 8

Allen is holding the cards in his two hands. They are trying to jump out of his hands. I can see his muscles holding tight.

"Ha. Ha. He's not coming back," Wyatt laughed.

"So you think it's funny that we are out in the middle of nowhere by ourselves?" Allen spat.

I don't think Wyatt is funny laughing. I think he is scared laughing.

"I want my mom," Monica said.

Monica is still standing, but she isn't jumping so much now...just bouncing a little.

"AH!" Allen yelped.

"WHOOSH!"

The cards jumped out of Allen's hands.

Krista is looking at the cards. She picked up the box!

"The game is called 'ENDURE,'" Krista said.

I don't know what that word means. I hope I am not the only one.

"What does endure mean?" Monica asked Krista.

Good. I know I couldn't say that word.

"Ha! Endure is to withstand hardship or stress. We're dead. Ha!" Wyatt cackled.

I do not know what the first words Wyatt said mean, but I got the 'we're dead.'

"Stop it, Wyatt! You're scaring Troy and Monica," snapped Krista.

"Ha! You think *they're* scared. Look at Allen."

Allen is as white as Wyatt and his mouth is open like it is filled up with an invisible sock.

"To endure just means you don't give up. You keep going even when you're tired. Endurance—we all have that from karate," said Krista.

I had two lessons. Hold up two fingers for Krista. Two. "Ew."

"You only had two lessons, Troy? You'll just have to learn faster than everyone else."

Fast? I never did fast.

"Listen, the box says, 'ENDURE - Will you be Predator, Prey or Protector?'" said Krista.

I don't know those words. Well, I know protector. My mom says that all the time. She protects me from the cold, and getting sick and getting hurt and-

"ZZZZZZ!"

What is that buzzing? It's the cards. They are shaking and jumping.

"AHHH!" Krista screamed.

The cards are jumping on Krista!

"The cards are getting her! Ha!" said Wyatt.

"Take them off of her! Help me!" Allen yelled.

Allen is grabbing the cards and pulling them off
Krista. So is Wyatt. Monica is jumping in circles. And
I...am just standing here. Am I supposed to do
something? The cards keep jumping back on Krista.
She's screaming. "They are stinging! Get them off of me."
I am just standing here. Krista is falling on the
ground. Her face is covered with the cards. Allen and
Wyatt are throwing the cards off fast and the cards are
jumping back on faster. She is screaming. "Help me!" I
can hear Sal the shark's voice. It is yelling real loud
inside my head. Deal the cards! Deal the cards! Deal the
cards!
I will pick up a card. Hold it. It is not jumping
back. Give Monica a card. It is not jumping back. Give
Wyatt a card. He threw it. Try again. Hold this. "Ol is!"
"What, Troy?" asked Wyatt.
Hold this! "Ol is!"
"HA! It's not jumping back," answered Wyatt.
Put a card in Allen's pocket. Give me a card. Give
Monica a card. Give Wyatt a card. Put a card in Krista's
hand.
"They stopped," Allen gasped.
Allen is right. The cards are falling off Krista. The
buzzing stopped. They are moving into a little pile.
Krista is sitting up. Hand her a card.
"Troy's right," said Krista. "We have to play the
game."
How? "Ow?"
"I don't know, Troy. All it says on the box is
'predator, prey or protector,'" Krista said. "How many
cards does everyone have in their hand?"

I have four. Hold up four fingers.

"Four," Allen said.

"Ha! Four!" said Wyatt.

"Right, and Monica has four and so do I," said Krista. "There is the stack on the ground. I'll go first. I will pick this card from my hand. It's a flamingo."

Feathers. Krista is growing pink feathers.

"What's happening to me?" Krista whispered.

"Monica, it's your turn. Pick a card."

"I picked a monkey," Monica said.

A brown tail is coming out of Monica's butt.

"My turn," said Allen. "An alligator."

Allen is turning green. I don't want to play this game.

"Ha! I'll pick a card from the stack. It's a crab!" Wyatt said.

"POP!"

Wyatt turned into a white crab. He is talking.

"Allen, don't eat me. I'm too easy. Eat everyone else!" said Wyatt.

"What are you talking about?" Allen asked.

"Ha! You'll find out!" Wyatt said.

"Where's Wyatt going?" Monica asked.

Wyatt is running toward the big water.

"SPLASH!"

He just jumped into the water!

"Go get him!" Monica yelled.

"I'm not going in that water. Look how rough it is," Allen said.

Allen is right. There are lots of rocks and the water is moving very fast.

"Just keep playing the game. He'll come back," Krista said.

Yes. He probably just needed a drink.

"Pick a card, Troy," Krista said.

Krista has more feathers and her legs are getting skinny.

No! "OO!" Shake my head no. I am not playing this game.

"Pick a card! You have to play! Rrrr!" Allen snarled.

Allen has a long mouth and big teeth. Monica is a monkey. Krista is a big pink bird that stands on one leg. I am not picking a card. "WHOOSH!" A card jumped up and stuck to me. It says P-R-E-Y.

"It's says prey," Krista chirped.

I am praying—a lot.

"Troy, I think I know what this game is. Hurry up and pick a card from your hand, or the Endure game will pick it for you," Krista said.

I am not picking.

"Hurry up, Troy, and pick something big! I have to fly away soon. Look at Allen!"

Allen is an alligator. He is not moving. His eyes are staring hard at Krista.

"Hurry, Troy!" yelled Krista.

Allen is sliding toward Krista.

"SNAP!"

CHAPTER 9

"Pick, Troy!" Krista is flying away. Allen tried to bite her, but he missed. Allen is looking at Monica and me. What card should I pick?

"SNAP!"

OOPS! Allen ate all of my cards. "WHOA!" Monica is pulling me away. We are going toward a tree. Allen is moving at us.

"THUNK!" A rock hit Allen on the head.

"KIII!" Krista the bird! She dropped a rock on Allen's head from up in the sky.

"Hurry, Troy!" Monica monkey is pulling me. "Climb the tree!"

Monica is trying to pull me up but she is a small monkey. I am up a little. "Hold on to the tree, Troy!"

Monica let go of me and ran up the tree. Hold on. I am holding on. Don't let go of the tree. Allen is sliding closer to me. Monica is coming back with a stick. I have to hold on.

"SNAP!" Allen is trying to bite my feet. He can almost reach me. "THUNK!" Monica is hitting him with a stick so he won't get me. Wow. Monica is getting bigger. Every time she hits Allen with the stick it looks like she grows a little bit. She is spinning the stick around very fast. OOPS! She dropped it.

"SNAP!" Uh oh oh, Allen ate the stick.

"Come on, Troy! Pull up!" Monica screamed.

I am moving up. Monica is as big as me now. I have to climb. She is helping me. Up. One more branch up. Sit down. Monica is breathing very loud. So am I. Allen is still trying to climb up the tree. "SNAP!" He bit the tree.

"I want to go home, Troy," Monica said.

I think we have to finish playing this game first. Monica's mom might not want a pet.

"SNAP!"

I know Allen's mom won't like a pet. They don't even have a pool.

"Flutter!"

It's Krista bird. Hey, she looks bigger, too. Not a real lot bigger...just a little bigger. Hi, Krista. "I Issa."

"I think I have an idea how this game works," chirped Krista.

Me too...if you lose an alligator eats you. I will make an alligator mouth with my arms. Snap! "Rrrr!"

"I know Allen might eat us, Troy. But if this is a game, we have to figure out what the goal is...and we have to find Sensei Dennis."

I hope he didn't lose the paper with the rules. I lose parts of my games a lot.

"Maybe Sensei Dennis is over there." Monica pointed.

Over there, far away, is a big mountain. Some of the trees on it are on fire.

"We should go and find him." Monica bounced.

I want to fly like Krista. Maybe she can get me a card? Point to the cards on the ground. "Ars!"

"You want a card, Troy?" asked Krista.

Yes! "Es!"

"Let me try to get one."

Krista is flying down to the ground. Allen is turning to look at her.

"Allen! Don't eat Krista!" Monica screamed.

"Allen, wake up in there! Don't listen to Wyatt! You don't want to eat us!" Monica is yelling.

Allen is still looking at Krista.

"Allen, remember what Sensei Dennis said. "Be flexible! Change your mind!"

Allen is looking around like he doesn't know what to do.

Allen is not chasing Krista. She got one! Krista got a card. Allen is smelling the air. Oh no! He's chasing after Krista.

"Fly away, Krista!" Monica yelled.

Uh oh oh! There is another alligator in front of Krista. Allen is leaping at Krista. Oh no!

"WHACK!"

Allen knocked the other alligator away. The other alligator is growling at Allen. "RRRR!" Allen jumped up in the air. "SNAP!" He is chasing the other alligator away. Yes! The other alligator is all gone. Krista and

Allen are just looking at each other. Allen is growing a little bit bigger.

"Allen, are you in there?" Krista asked.

"I think it's me. I feel really...hungry," Allen said.

I have gummies. "Uh-ies." Pull them out of my pocket. Throw them down to Allen.

"CHOMP!"

They are all gone. Allen was very hungry. Maybe now he won't eat us for a while.

"Thanks, Troy," Allen said.

Allen said thanks to me. Maybe he won't throw me off the lunch table again. I wish I had more gummies.

"I have a card for you, Troy," Krista said.

Krista has a card in her beak. It is an elephant.

"Wait! Don't take it, Troy. You should be dealt a whole new hand since I ate your last one," Allen said.

Monica is jumping up.

"I'll deal it," Monica said. "You guys don't have any fingers. Here you go, Troy...one, two, three, four cards. Now you can pick your favorite animal."

I don't want to be an animal. I want to be Troy. The cards are shaking in my hands. I can see the animals moving around. A snake, a big kind of cat with spots, an elephant and a—

"RUN"! yelled Dennis.

It's Sensei Dennis! He is grabbing me. Krista is flying away. Wow, alligators can run fast. Allen is right next to us. Monica jumped on Dennis's back and he is holding both of us. Sensei looks bigger and his has a red and blue dragon tail and wings are on his back. I hear growling.

"RRR!"

It's getting closer. Where is Chad? Maybe Sensei couldn't catch him.

"RRRR!"

Tigers are chasing us. Stop. We stopped. Uh oh oh. Tigers are all around. They are little, skinny tigers, but there are lots of them. One, two, three…ten of them. They are in a big circle around us. One is stepping in.

"WHOOSH!"

Sensei Dennis blew a big fire breath at him. The one tiger ran away. The others ones are stepping backward a little. They stopped. They are not running away.

"Nobody move," Dennis whispered.

The tigers are moving closer.

"WHOOOOOOOOSH!"

Sensei Dennis is blowing fire at the grass all around us in a big circle.

"That will hold them back for a minute" Dennis said. "Troy, where are your cards?"

I pull them out and show him.

"FLAP!"

Krista is flying over us. Dennis is yelling up to her.

"Krista, you have to play a different bird card. You have to help us. Pick a different card!"

Krista is pulling a card out of her wing. Her color is changing. Her head is turning all white and her wings are so big. I never saw a bird with wings that big.

"Krista's a pretty white bird!" Monica shrieked.

"She's an albatross," said Dennis.

"How can she help us?" asked Allen.

"This is a game...she has to figure that out," Dennis said.

"KIII!" Krista shrieked at the tiger. He isn't scared! He's chasing her. Fly fast, Krista! She got away from him.

"SWOOP!"

Krista flew down and grabbed Monica. Krista is flying away with Monica!

"RRRR!"

A tiger jumped over the fire. "WHAM!" Sensei Dennis kicked him so hard the tiger spun around. Dennis is grabbing his tail. "SWISH!" He threw the tiger far away. "WHOOSH!" Sensei Dennis blew out more fire, but the tigers are getting closer.

"SNAP!" Allen is snapping at the tigers. They are coming. Sensei Dennis is holding me and blowing fire at the tigers. There are lots of them. WOW! Dennis kicked away a tiger jumping on Allen's back. More tigers are coming at – "WHOOOOOA!"

CHAPTER 10

I'm up in the air! I am flying away from the tigers.
Krista has me in her bird claws. So far I am doing pretty
good at this game. I can see Allen and Dennis down
there. They are fighting the tigers. Sensei Dennis is
really going fast when he is not holding me. Allen is
watching all the tigers, then real fast he gets one.

"You alright, Troy?"

Yes! "Es." Krista is a very big albatross bird now.

"I'm going to put you up on the mountain with
Monica! Then I'm going back for Allen!"

Wow! Krista made us a big nest out of purple
flowers. Monica is sitting in it, up in a tree. PLOP!
Ouch! Now I am in the nest. Krista is flying away.

"Wasn't that fun, Troy?!" Monica cheered.

Fun? She looks like she wants me to say yes. Nod
yes.

"How come you don't talk?"

Oh boy. I don't know. Lift my shoulders and hold
my hands up.

"You don't know?"
Nod no.
"Is it hard for you to make words?"
Nod yes.
"Can you make sounds?"
I can. I can make lots of sounds. Nod yes!
"Really? So can I! I can be a telephone. Ring! Ring!" said Monica.

That was not very good. I can do all the sounds from my Dad's phone he carries around. Pretend to hold a phone to my ear. "Deedle leep! Baloop! Dum, dum, dum, dummm! Brnnng! La dad da!"

"A cell phone!" Monica guessed.

Monica is laughing! I can do more sounds. Here is the man who lives across the street's motorcycle: "Bvrooom! Bvrooom! Bvrooom! Brrrrr..."

"A motorcycle! That was good, Troy!"

Monica has a pretty laugh. I hope she turns back into a girl. "Pop! Pop! Pop!"

"Popcorn! My mom makes popcorn at home...it's my favorite..." said Monica.

Quiet. That did not make Monica laugh. The popcorn made her sad.

"I'm scared, Troy. I want my mom."

Monica is crying. If Monica's mom was here, she would put her arm on her shoulder. That is what you do if someone cries. I will put my arm on Monica's shoulder. Her body is shaking.

"Thanks, Troy. Can you do popcorn again?"
"Pop! Pop. Pop..."

Monica is going to sleep. She feels nice and warm. I hope she turns back into a girl soon. I don't know how to make the sound of a banana.

CHAPTER 11

The tree is shaking. Where is Monica? I don't see her. Monica?

"Wake up, Troy!"

Monica is jumping behind my head.

"Wake up, Troy! Look...the sun is up! It's blue!"

Monica is right. The sun is sky color blue, and the sky is yellow. Is other stuff backwards here? Where is Krista? "Isa?"

"She's not here yet. I'm hungry."

Me, too.

"Let's go find breakfast."

I would like to do that if I can get down from here. I can see a lot from up here. There is a lot of land and water is all around it. I see some roads and mountains and I see dragon's eyes. Take off my karate uniform. The dragon on the back. Oh, this place looks like the dragon. That is funny.

"Come on, Troy! Climb down!"

Monica is at the bottom. I think I want to be a monkey. Maybe I should pick a card? Hmm...

"SQUAWK!"

"Hurry up, Troy...get out of the nest!"

Birds are coming! Big ones! Put on my dragon uniform. Climb over the side. Climb down real careful. Hold on.

"SQUAWK!"

"AHHH!" I'm falling! I'm falling on rocks!

"BOUNCE!"

I hit the rocks and I am bouncing up, and down, and up and down. I stopped.

"Wasn't that fun, Troy?! The rocks are bouncy like a bed!"

I am glad rocks are backwards here—soft, not hard. The birds are landing in the nest. They are green and have mean faces. Does that mean they are nice? Where are their feathers?

"Shhh! Oh, I don't have to tell you that. I'm the noisy one. They are just baby dragons...I don't think they will hurt us.

Dragons? Oh...

"I saw some trees with fruit over there. Let's go quietly," Monica said.

The dragons are looking at us. I hope they are not hungry for monkeys or Troys.

"Bananas!"

Monica is right...it is a tree of bananas, all different colors. She is opening one. The insides are colors, too—pink and green and blue.

"Eat one, Troy. They taste good."

She is right. They are good. Maybe the baby dragons would like some. I will throw them one.

"PLOP!"

That was not high.

"Troy, are you trying to feed the dragons?" asked Monica.

Nod yes.

"Here, I will help you."

Monica is spinning the bananas in her hand.

"FLING!"

That went in the nest.

They are eating it! Give Monica some more.

"Hey, Troy, they like them!" laughed Monica.

It's snowing up.

"Look at the snow, Troy! It's coming from the ground."

Monica is bouncing more than ever. Bounce.

"Ounce?" I put my hands up in the 'I don't know' way.

"You want to know why I bounce all the time?" asked Monica. "I bounce because I have to hurry up!"

Hurry up and do what? I look at Monica with the 'huh?' eyes.

"You have to hurry up! Or you'll be late. You have to hurry up and decide what to do. You have to hurry up and go! You just have to hurry up, Troy."

Monica is not like me at all. I am okay wherever I am. I don't have to go somewhere else.

"Like now! We have to hurry up and find Sensei!"

Oh. I thought he would find us.

"Look, the snow is sticking to the bottom of the branches," Monica said. "Look how fast I can swing from

this branch! WHOA!" Monica's hands slipped off the branch.

"THUMP!" She fell down in the snow. Uh oh oh, some snow is coming to us. It is like something is swimming to us under the snow. Hmm...

"A SHARK!" Monica screamed.

I can see the shark's eyes. It's Sal! I will hurry up now.

"Pick a card fast, Troy!" Monica said.

Oh, the cards. Which pocket did I put them in?

"Hurry up. The shark's coming!"

Monica is grabbing in my pockets.

"Here...pick this one, Troy. It's fast!"

OOPS! It dropped on the ground. It's the cat with spots. It says C-H-E-E-T-A-H. I don't know...

"Take it! Hurry up!"

Monica is picking it up. Uh oh oh...Monica has spots. "POOF!" The card is gone. Monica is not a monkey now. Monica is the C-H-E-E-T-A-H.

"Jump on my back, Troy!"

Get on Monica's back. Hold on.

"ZOOM!"

Wow! Monica can really hurry up! So can the shark. He is chasing us. The snow is getting higher and lower. A shark is fast in the snow. Too fast.

"CHOMP!"

A giant alligator jumped on the shark. It's Allen! He is so big!

"SWAT!"

He swatted the shark with his tail. The shark is sliding down the hill.

"Troy, I can't run anymore," Monica huffed.

Monica is lying down in the snow. Hmm...the snow is warm. Allen is coming over. He is so big now.

Monica is tired. She is breathing very loud. I will hold her...paw.

"Troy, who's the cheetah?" Allen asked.

Monica. "On-i-a."

"What are you saying, Troy?"

Allen doesn't understand me. Jump up and down like Monica does and point.

"What?"

Allen is not watching good.

"I don't have time for this. Where's Monica?"

Point.

"That's Monica?! Why didn't you tell me?" Allen snapped.

I did.

"Hurry up and put her on my back. I'll get her some water. You'd better ride, too. You'll be too slow," barked Allen.

I guess it is good that I can't talk, because I want to say something that is not nice.

Allen's back is hard and has lots of lines in it. Where is everybody, Allen? "Ea- is e o y?"

"What are you saying, Troy? Are you hungry or what?" Allen asked.

Allen doesn't understand me at all. He does not like trying to guess. Where is Krista? Here is a lake.

"Take a drink, Monica," said Allen.

I will help Monica get some water. Put it in my hand. She is licking it.

"I know how this game works, Troy," said Allen. "Sensei Dennis told me it's all about—"

"BZZZZZZZ!"

"AHHHH!" A giant pointy bug is flying at my head. I will hurry up away!

"BZZZZ!"

"No, Allen...don't!" I think I heard Sensei Dennis.

"SNAP! I got the bug, Troy," Allen smiled. "It won't bite—"

"POOF!"

Allen is gone.

CHAPTER 12

"What happened to Allen?" Monica asked.

She seems all better now. I will have to show her. Stretch my arms out.

"He got real big?"

Nod yes. Then, "OOF"!

"Then he blew up?"

Nod yes.

"Now he's all gone?"

Nod yes.

"What should we do now?" asked Monica.

We have to find the rules of the game. I know one rule: if you help protect someone, you get bigger. But if you do it too many times you go away like 'POOF!' I wonder where they go? If this is like my video game you go to the next level if you do good. Rules. "Ules!"

"The rules? Do you know where they are, Troy?"

Nod no.

"Troy, look at the Dragon on your back! It looks like this place."

I know. That is funny.

"Wow, Troy. This place is shaped just like the dragon. We are down here by the tail. We can use it like a map! Can you see that?"

Oh...now I see.

"I think we should go up to the head part. The head must know the rules."

Oh. That is a good idea.

This is a far walk. It stopped snowing. The snow is water now. I hope there are no more sharks.

"ROAR!"

I hear a tiger.

"A tiger is coming. Troy, I can run fast, but you have to pick a card," Monica whispered.

I have a snake, an elephant...oh, a card like Monica...a C-H-E-E-T-A-H. I will pick it. Take the card.

"POP!"

Wow. I feel like worms are crawling all over me and stuff is popping out of my skin. It's fur—fur with spots. Inside my muscles are scrunching up. Ow! My bones are moving around inside me. Uh oh oh! My teeth...they are all pointy. A tail! I have a tail. I always wanted one of those.

"The tigers are coming!" Monica yelled.

Monica is running away. I should run, too, this time!

Wow! I can catch Monica.

"Keep running, Troy...they are still coming!" Monica yelled.

I am so fast! This is great. Look at me! I wish Dad could see. I can run faster than a tiger! They would let me stay on the soccer team now! What is that sound? I never heard that coming from my mouth before. It is my breathing and it is very loud like air coming out of a balloon. My insides hurt. I do not want to run anymore.

"ROAR!"

A tiger is getting close to us. I run up the hill. I have to keep going... Monica is getting ahead of me. Keep running... My legs hurt me. The tiger is getting closer. Jump over the rocks. Monica jumped in the water. "Jump in, Troy!"

The tiger is coming! I can't jump in water. I will run the other way. Then he will chase me and he won't get Monica. Keep running. He ran past me. The tiger jumped in the water! Tigers are good swimmers. He is catching Monica... NO!

Everything is yelling at me from inside my head. Run away! Water is scary! You can't breathe in water! The tiger isn't chasing me anymore. Don't move. The tiger is catching Monica. Do something! Don't do anything! Do Something! Run away! Help Monica!

The tiger is fast. He is close to Monica. Monica is swimming. Her head is going in the water. The tiger is opening his mouth. He bit her tail!

Jump! I am on the tigers back! He is shaking his head. He is pulling Monica. Hit his head! He won't let go of Monica. Hit his head. Hit his head with my paw.

"ROAR!"

Ouch! My bones are stretching. My paw is getting bigger. Hit the tiger with my big paw. It's even bigger. He won't let go of Monica. Rocks. NO!

"WHACK!" Monica's head hit a rock.

"SMASH!" I hit the tiger HARD! He let go of Monica's tail.

I am getting wetter. The tiger is going under the water. The water is on my chin. The tiger...he is gone. I can swim. Cheetahs can swim better than Troys. I can swim fast. I am catching up to Monica. Her head is going under the water. There is water everywhere. The land is far away. I will bite Monica's neck—not too hard—like the mommy cats do when they pick up their baby kittens. Wake up, Monica! I am bigger than Monica. I have to swim. Keep swimming. Keep swimming. Keep swimming...

CHAPTER 13

My head keeps going under the water. Aaah!
Water is in my mouth. Monica, wake up. I can't keep
holding Monica out of the water. If I let go of her, maybe I
can swim and get help. But she will go under the water.
Cheetahs can't breathe under water. Where are my
cards? In my fur? Here they are. Does Monica have
some cards in her fur? Yes! Here! Put this card in her
mouth. No, it's slipping away. Monica, put it in your
mouth. These paw hands don't work as good as Troy
hands. Monica, here, take the card... She bit it! Oh. The
fur is falling off of her. Her skin is getting slippery. She
has fins. Ah! Water squirted in my face out of a hole in
her back. I am getting bigger... POP!

CHAPTER 14

"So, Troy, you made it to level two."

Mr. G? Why is my school principal here? He looks a little different here. His eyebrows are real long and his face and hands are bright yellow. Oh, and I am Troy again. No fur. This is a new place. A big square we are in. It is kind of yellow, with a soft floor like grass. It has a roof, but no walls. It is like a day outside when there are no clouds and no rain and mom says, 'let's go for a walk in the park.' I never want to do that. I can stay inside and play video games...it does not matter what kind of outside day it is.

They are here! Sensei Dennis, Krista, Allen, Chad and Wyatt. They are all standing on the yellow square doing karate. Where is Monica?

Principal G is looking at me and his face is changing colors again. It's purple now.

"Troy, now that you have made it to level two, you must train for the next level," said Mr. G.

Train? No special extra games for making it to the next level? No star? This sounds like work. What about Monica? "O-ca?"

"Monica should be here soon. Let us begin," said G.

"Master G, I'll work with Allen and Troy. They aren't ready for you. You can work with the team kids," said Sensei Dennis.

"Why do you say that?" asked Master G.

"Krista, Chad and Wyatt have special talent. You could do more with them," said Sensei Dennis.

Mr. G is leaning toward Sensei Dennis. "I am a martial arts teacher. If someone wants to learn I teach them."

That leaves me out.

"I'm sorry. I just meant that Allen and Troy will slow the class down a little," whispered Sensei Dennis.

Sensei Dennis is talking low, but I can tell what he is saying by the way his lips move.

"It's easy to coach people with certain talent and make them great. A great instructor can bring out the best in everyone," Mr. G said.

Uh oh oh... Mr. G is coming to me. "Troy, would you like to learn how to be faster and stronger?"

I think this is a trick. But he is looking right at my face and my head is nodding yes.

"When someone is just starting like Troy, it is better for him to learn how to focus one move." Mr. G is holding my hand up. I am going to show you a 'palm.' Just push your arm straight like you are pushing a big button."

I can push a button.

"Good. You did it. Again...and again. Now you see this piece of paper? The button is on the other side. So push right through this paper and push the button."

"POP!"

I split the paper right in half. I am stronger already.

"Very good, Troy. Now a piece of paper is just a very thin wood board. So keep practicing pushing the button and soon you will break right through a board."

I can do this. Push the button. Push the button. Push the button.

"That's the way, Troy." Allen is standing next to me. "I can't do all that fancy stuff like Chad and Wyatt. But I can do a good side kick, and if I just do it over and over more than anybody else, I will be great at it and no one will beat me."

Push the button. Push the button.

"You want to know my other secret?" whispered Allen. "I watch. I watch them over and over. See them sparring over there?"

Mr. G is being the judge person and Chad and Wyatt are sparring. They are throwing lots of kicks.

"I just keep watching them. So when they try to jump up and throw a fancy move, I will see it coming. Then when I get my chance...BOOM! Side kick!" said Allen.

Mr. G is talking loud to Chad and Wyatt. "The score is twenty-five for Chad to twenty-three for Wyatt. Can either of you tell me the object of sparring?"

"Sure," said Chad. "It's to score on the other guy."

"No!" snapped Mr. G. "It's not to get scored on yourself. You have let Wyatt score on you twenty-five times, and if he had focus and power in his moves it would have been more."

Now Mr. G is turning to Wyatt. "You, Wyatt, have been scored on twenty three times! And if Chad wasn't so wild and had not missed with so many kicks it would have been more... Everyone come over here. We are going to work on evasion."

What does that mean?

"Come on over, Troy and Allen. Mr. G is working on drills to move so you don't get hit," said Sensei Dennis.

I will go. I do not want to get hit. I will learn *evasion*.

Mr. G showed us how to move around when someone tries to grab you. He kept showing me how to step with my feet so I don't trip. Maybe when I get good at that, I could play in other sports, too. Push the button. Push the button. Now Allen is next to me doing his side kick over and over and I am pushing the button. Mr. G is watching us.

"Keep going, gentlemen. I do not fear the opponent with ten thousand moves. I fear the opponent that practices one move ten thousand times," said Mr. G.

"Alright," said Allen. "Only nine thousand, nine hundred fifty-one to go."

Push the button. Push the button. Uh oh oh! "AAAH!"

"What's wrong, Troy?" asked Allen.

I'm leaking! Rain is coming out of my hands. Point to my hands.

"What?" asked Allen.

Point to my hands again.

"That's just sweat, Troy. It happens when you work hard."

Oh. I never did that before.

"Troy, Allen...come here. It's time to find out about some of the rules," said Sensei Dennis.

CHAPTER 15

"There are three levels. One way to get to the next level is by helping your team. Every time you help a team member, you grow. Once you have helped enough players, you pop to the next level," said Sensei Dennis.

He is telling me about the game now. Before he told me all of us had to do a karate lesson with Principal G. Here they call him Master G. I learned some different kicks and what to do if somebody twists your arms behind your back. It wasn't too hard...you just turn the right way and untwist yourself.

"So you win by being the protector? Why is Chad here? He just ran away," asked Krista.

"That's what you think of me?" asked Chad.

"Chad didn't just run away. He caused the tigers to chase him, and got them away from all of you. That's how he got here," said Sensei Dennis.

"How did Wyatt get here? He never helps anyone," said Allen.

"Ha! There's more than one way to move up a level...if you're smart enough to figure it out," said Wyatt.

"There are secret passages. Many are under water. Wyatt managed to find the first one, and he had the right card. Only certain creatures could get through that passage alive," answered Sensei Dennis.

"You can die here?" asked Krista.

"No, but you can get stuck here—for a very long time—and forget who you are. Tigers are people who are stuck. If you don't make it through a level, the game will keep popping you back to right where we started."

"How do we get out of this game?" asked Allen.

"If you move up three levels, it will pop you back to the real world for a while."

"Wait. What do you mean 'for a while?' I don't want to play this anymore! This is no good! I'm never coming back here again! This place stinks!" yelled Allen.

Yes, it has too many smells.

"You can get out of the game, but the game never gets out of you," said Sensei Dennis.

"This is crazy! I can't spend the rest of my life playing games!" screamed Krista.

The rest of my life playing games? That would be like a good dream!

"It could get worse," said Sensei Dennis.

He is speaking real low now, like it is something he doesn't want somebody else to hear...but we are the only somebodies around.

Sensei Dennis is looking right at us. "Sal is back in the game. He is powerful here, but he can't control the game because he is out of balance."

"What is that supposed to mean?" Allen asked.

"Ha! Balance...you don't know anything. Nature has to always have balance between earth, wind, fire and water. Otherwise things get all messed up. Sal has too much water. He's a shark. So he needs to team up with wind, like Krista when she's a bird, and earth, like the land animals, and fire, like Sensei Dennis when he's a dragon," said Wyatt.

"Wyatt's right. You can close this game down as a team. But Sal doesn't want to close it down. He wants to control it all by himself, and he is trying to do that by bringing more and more water here. At home he is just a regular guy, but here he is king of the water," said Sensei Dennis.

"Where is he bringing the water from?" asked Krista.

"From our earth," said Sensei Dennis.

"He can't do that," said Allen.

"He can and he is," said Sensei Dennis. "I was assembling a team of top black belts to come here and help me get this game back in balance. One of them, the tiger, cheated and gave the game to Sal.

"Wait, you mean if he wins, he will steal all the water from Earth?" asked Allen.

"Yes, that's exactly what I mean," said Dennis.

Hmm... No water... I would not have to take any more baths.

"Why can't Master G stop him?" asked Krista.

"Master G is the rules of the game. That duty was passed down to him by his ancestors. He can't play. He can only teach. He goes wherever the game pops up. I

found the game in a shop in China town. I gave it to
Sensei Sal as a birthday gift. When he opened the box we
found out what it really was. Sal and I were sucked into
the game. We reached the top levels and became what we
are now. Then Sal changed. He just wanted more and
more power. The game reveals your inner spirit. Now we
are stuck together, unless...

CHAPTER 16

Monica still isn't here. Sensei Dennis told us that someone has to go back through the secret passage Wyatt found. Then they have to find Monica and bring her back. After that we all have to reach the top level together to close down this game. We are picking cards to see who goes back for Monica.

"Look, only a small sea creature can get through the passage Wyatt found. Whoever has the right card can take Wyatt's crab card, because it was already played, and give it to Monica so she can get through the passage. Let's see your cards," said Sensei Dennis.

Krista is pulling out her cards. "I have a bull, a gorilla and a hawk. Does that mean I can't go and help Monica?"

"Sorry, you can't," said Sensei Dennis.

"Ha, I can't go. All my cards are reptiles—a snake, a frog and an iguana. They'll drown," laughed Wyatt.

"I'll go. I have a whale. Maybe whales eat sharks," said Chad.

"Ha! Give me that! Wyatt grabbed the card. "A whale is a mammal…you'll drown," laughed Wyatt. "Plus, whales mainly eat plankton, the smallest creatures in the ocean."

Plankton, I don't have one of those cards.

"I can go! I have a shark! I'll eat Sal right up!" Allen said.

"A shark is too big to get through the passage," said Sensei Dennis.

"Why can't you pick a card and go, Sensei?" asked Krista.

"When Sal the shark, along with the tiger, and an old friend (who was the eagle) and I reached the top level together, we were supposed to jump out of the game together. Then it would close down and we would be free of it forever. Instead, when the rest of us jumped out, Sal stayed behind to gather power. Now I will always be the dragon until I can form a team to jump out of the top level together. "The team must represent all of the elements—earth, wind, water and fire," said Sensei Dennis. "Then the game will be shut down and everyone in it will be free."

"What happened to your friend the eagle?" asked Krista.

"I wish I knew. I haven't seen her since that day," said Sensei Dennis.

"Troy, you're the only one left. Let's see your cards," said Allen.

I will show my cards…an elephant, a snake and an…octopus. Uh oh oh…

CHAPTER 17

Water is everywhere around me. I am just turning over and over and over. My eight legs are going everywhere. It's funny trying to move them. There are so many, they don't go where I want them to. That sometimes happens with my regular legs. Water is in my face and mouth and eyes, but it doesn't hurt me like when I am Troy. I am not choking when water gets in my mouth, it just washes right out.

Sensei Dennis put me in the water real nice. I tried to hold on to him, but I don't know how to use all these legs good. The water just sucked me down, like when I lose a little soap down the drain. The water is pushing forward and I can see some fish. I hope none of them like to eat octopus. I stopped spinning around. Now I am just kind of floating.

I have to find out how to use all these legs. I think I need to go that way. Let's see…if I move these legs… No, that just makes me spin in a circle. I will just try one leg at a time. Okay, if I kind of paddle I can move this way. Where is Monica? I hope she is still a dolphin, or how will I know her?

Oh No! Lots of fish. They don't look like nice fish. They have pointy teeth. Paddle, paddle, hide under the rock.

I can't stay way down here. Wyatt told me dolphins play at the top so they can get some air. I think the pointy teeth fish went away. How do I get up to the top? These legs are not going the right way. If I was a balloon, I would just go up to the top. Maybe if I just act like a balloon, I will go up there. Okay, I will blow my head up. It's working. Up, up, up, I'm on top! AHH! Choking. Air is in my mouth, it's making me cough. Go under the water.

If I put my eyes up and don't get air in my mouth, I can see. Where are you, Monica? Water. Every way I look, I see water. No other stuff...just water.

"SPLASH!"

Dolphins! There are a bunch of them jumping. Wow! The fish are swimming fast away. Why? Why is everybody swimming away? Wait, everyone is running away. Then I will run away! Paddle, paddle, paddle. I am going the same way as everyone else, but not as fast. Uh oh oh, I see a shark. It's Sal! He is chasing a little fish. His mouth is opening way up. He is going to chomp it!

"THUMP!"

It's Monica. She knocked Sal away from the little fish. Sal is mad. He's chasing Monica. No! He is going to chomp her! I wish I had more karate lessons. Wait, I know. Paddle, Paddle, Paddle.

"CHOMP!"

He missed her. I have to go fast. Wrap around. I will wrap all my legs around Sal's head. He can't open his mouth. WHOA! He is throwing his head all around. I will hold on tight. Don't let go.

"You got him, Troy!" said Monica.

I am holding on. Sal is trying to shake me off.

"What are you going to do now?" asked Monica.

Oh. I have to do something else?

"Troy, you're getting bigger," said Monica.

Oh, good! Oh, not good! I won't fit through the tunnel. I can squeeze Sal tighter. Tighter! Tighter!

"POOF!"

Sal is gone. I think he went back to the start of the game.

CHAPTER 18

Monica and I squeezed back through the tunnel. Now we are back with everyone.

"The next level is much more difficult. The creatures are bigger, faster and stronger," said Sensei Dennis.

"Sensei, the best strategy would be to leave Troy and Monica here. They will slow us down. We would be at the top level by now if we weren't waiting for them. Ha!" Wyatt smirked.

"Shut up, Wyatt! We aren't leaving anyone," yelled Allen.

"Ha! I am just calculating our best odds, and our best chance is without the added drag of two players who can't keep up," snickered Wyatt.

I can keep up. I am not staying here! Everyone is not running away without me! Throw!

"WHACK!"

"Ouch!" You hit me with a rock!" Wyatt groaned.

I threw the rock at Wyatt.

"Stop being a baby, Wyatt. The rocks are soft," said Chad.

"Wow, I never saw Troy get so upset before. Troy, are you Okay?" asked Krista.

"Good for you, Troy. Wyatt deserved that!" said Allen.

"At least he's finally paying attention," smirked Wyatt.

Throw!

"Bonk!"

That hit Wyatt in the nose.

"He definitely deserved that," said Allen.

Uh oh oh. Wyatt is picking up a rock.

"BONK!"

That hit Allen.

Uh oh oh! Everyone is picking up rocks.

"STOP!" Sensei Dennis commanded. "We have to get to the next level. All of us."

"Ow?" How?

"By working as a team. We need to lift that statue back up," Sensei Dennis said pointing to a giant tree lying on the ground. The tree is longer than a railroad train and all kinds of stuff is cut into it.

"It's the symbol of the earth, the wind, the fire and the water. Sal took it down and put that up."

Wow! It's a shark; a giant shark made of water.

"Ha! He's done the impossible. Water is a liquid, so it *always* takes on the shape of whatever vessel it is poured into. His water statue defies the laws of physics. Somehow that water has determined its own shape."

"Which means Sal is getting stronger," said Krista.

"Let's get this up and even the score a little. Start grabbing those vines," said Sensei.

Sensei Dennis tied the vines around the tree, and hooked it around a bunch of other trees. Everyone is pulling on the vines except Monica and me. We are throwing rocks and branches under the tree every time it gets up a little higher, so that if they get tired the tree doesn't fall all the way back down. The tree is getting higher and higher.

"Come on, everybody...team work. One more pull... Heave!" Sensei Dennis yelled as the tree went straight up. It's kind of rocking around. It's going to fall! No!

It did not fall. It is standing up. I see pictures on the cut in the tree. Hmmm...one of them looks like me. Uh oh oh...what is that shaking?

The tree is on fire! And wind is blowing around it! 'SPLASH!"

The water shark just fell down.

"BOOOOOM!"

I can't see anything.

CHAPTER 19

I don't know how Sensei Dennis got us to this level.
But we are here. It is very purple here. The sky, the
ground and the clouds are all different colors of purple.
The trees have brown and purple leaves and green and
purple tree trunks. The purple rocks under my feet are
hard.

"What is this ugly place?" Krista asked.

"I don't know," said Wyatt.

He never said that before. He always knows.
Monica is just standing still. Very still.

"How come my legs are moving so slow?" Chad
asked.

"Here, you become what is opposite. Here, the land
doesn't change. In this place something about *you*
changes." Sensei Dennis is breathing ice out of his
mouth—no fire, just ice.

"Iwanttogohomenow!"

"What did you say, Troy?" asked Allen.

I think I just talked, real fast.

"IsaidIwanttogohomenow!"

"Shut up, Troy!" yelled Krista.

Why is Krista being mean to me? She is always nice. Uh oh oh.

"You all are going to have to reach inside here. We have to get across the purple field and climb the ladders to the next level," said Dennis.

Ice is dripping from Sensei's nose. My feet are wet.

"Sal is bringing in more water. Go!" Dennis said, nudging everyone forward.

I am going. Uh oh oh...where is everybody? Look around. Why are they way back there? Go get them. My legs are moving very fast. Wow!

"Troy, you are the fastest one here now. Don't wait for us! Get across the field and pull down the ladders," yelled Dennis.

"WHOOSH!"

"What's that?" asked Wyatt.

"It's wind. Look!" Monica pointed.

"Tornados! Lots of little tornados. Troy can't make it through them!" Allen screamed.

"Come on, just stay low and keep moving or we'll drown," said Dennis.

The water is touching my socks. Sensei Dennis is pushing my back. "GO!"

I am running.

"SPLASH!"

Fast, I am running so fast I am on top of the water.

"WHOOSH!"

The tornado things are coming!

"WHOOSH!"

It missed me.

"WHOOSH!"

That one missed me, too.

"WHOOSH!"

"AAAAAHHHH!"

I am spinning around and around! I am inside a tornado. The wind is so strong. I can't hear anyone! Dirt is getting in my eyes. My arms can't move. It is so loud inside my ears. I am upside down! Wind is in my nose. The air is stuck in my mouth. It won't go out...it won't come in. I am going away...

"SPLASH!"

I am wet. I think the wind threw me back in the water.

"Get up! Troy! Get up!" Everybody is back there yelling at me.

I have to push up, up. The water is at my knees. More tornados are coming. RUN!

I am running and running. I can see everyone running behind me, but they are going slow. My body is not tired. I can run and run. Ladders, I see ladders up that hill. Zip. I am up the hill. I think the ladders hook on to this purple bar. Yes, they do. Drop down the ladders into the water.

One.

"PLOP!"

Two.

"PLOP!"

Three.

"PLOP!"

Four.

"PLOP!"

The wind stopped. Yeah!

Uh oh oh...the water is coming. Run, everybody! They are not going very fast. The water is going to wash them away before they get to the ladders. I will do something fast! What?...

Maybe I could hook the ladders together and they will float across the water so everyone can reach. Should I do that? Yes! I have to do it right now! Go! Hook. Hook. Hook! The ladders are long. They are floating. I will climb down and get everyone up. Allen is here first. Monica is on his shoulders. The water is up to his neck.

"Troy, get Monica. She's so heavy," Allen gasped.

Pull Monica. Monica looks so sad.

"Monicayouaresopretty." OOPS!

"What did you say, Troy?"

"Monicayouaresopretty."

Uh oh oh. Did I say that? Words are just coming fast out of my mouth. I have to be careful. Cover up my mouth with my hand.

"Thank you," Monica said.

Monica is smiling at me. She is just looking at me and is not jumping and running somewhere else. Smile back. Oh, move my hand off my mouth. Smile.

"What are you doing, you idiots?! Get out of the way! Get up the ladder!" yelled Krista.

Krista is not nice here.

"Yo, is this the ladder? Cool." Wyatt is coming up the ladder.

Chad is still way back there. Sensei Dennis is pulling him forward. The water is getting high. Sensei Dennis is blowing on the water. It froze to ice! Sensei made a road of ice from all the way back where they are to the ladders. Dennis is sliding Chad across the ice. "HurryChadgettotheladder!" OOPS! Chad is slipping…

"SPLASH!"

Chad fell into the water. What is that? A shark is in the water. Uh oh oh…lots of sharks are in the water.

"SMASH!"

The big shark cut the ice with his fin. Sal! The big shark is Sal! Sensei Dennis is out floating on the ice. We have to help him. "Whatshouldwedo,Wyatt?"

"Haaa…I don't know."

"Whatshouldwedo,Allen?"

"Do you have any cards left, Troy?"

"No,Idonot."

Allen is turning to Krista. "Krista, do you have any cards left?"

"You can't have them! THEY'RE MINE!" Krista snapped.

Wow, Krista's voice is very strong.

"Ha, I have an extra card! Would you like it, Troy?" asked Wyatt.

Allen is grabbing the card. "Let me see that. An Orca whale? Can that beat a shark?"

"Ha, I forget…" said Wyatt.

"Come on, this place can't affect you that much," Allen screamed, grabbing Wyatt's shoulders.

"An Orca whale is also known as a killer whale, and has been observed attacking polar bears, seals, sea lions and sharks. HA! How did I know that?"

"Givemethecard!" Allen screamed.

I am not waiting. I am taking the card from Allen. The picture on it is a big whale. "OUCH!" I have a tail.

"WHOOSH!" There is a hole in my head. My arms are black fins and my belly is white. "OOPS!" I don't have any legs.

"SPLASH!"

I fell in the water.

Swim. I am swimming as fast as I can to Sensei. The sharks are making a circle around him. He is blowing ice at them, but they crack right through it. I am not scared of them. I am bigger than them. JUMP!

"SPLASH!"

The sharks are going back. Uh oh oh! They are coming again. I have to be scary. How?

I know. I will open my mouth and show them my big teeth. That is scary at the circus when the tigers do that.

"AAAAAH!"

It is working. They are scared. I never saw sharks get so scared. They are not coming in anymore. Swim under Sensei Dennis. He jumped on my back. GO!!!

Swim to the ladders!

"Hurry, Troy! Sal is right behind us!" Sensei screamed.

"CHOMP!"

"He just missed us, Troy! Quick, circle around. I have an idea!"

Swim around! Face Sal! He is big. His mouth is open—

"CHOM—"

"WHOOSH!"

Sensei Blew ice into Sal's jaws and now they are stuck open.

"Hurry, Troy. That won't last long."

Hurry. Swim away fast. Pick up Chad. Keep swimming.

We are here.

"Come on, everybody...pull Troy up on the ladder," Sensei Dennis yelled.

I am done being a whale. I want to be Troy now. Sleep.

CHAPTER 20

I feel warm. Open my eyes. Wow! The sky is just like at home, with regular white clouds and a yellow sun.

"Troy, you're okay. Can you get up? We're at the next level and we're going to train now," said Krista.

Krista is nice again.

"Ii—O." No! I can't talk again. My mouth is not going right. "Ew-OOO." No!

"Troy, what's wrong?"

I have to get up. No! My body is going slow again. NOOO!

"Troy, there are tears in your eyes," Krista said.

No. Turn my head. I am not getting up...ever.

"Ha! What's wrong with him?"

Monica is rubbing my shoulder. "Troy is sad."

"Ha! See? I told you he would slow us down," said Wyatt.

Allen put his chest up to Wyatt. "Be quiet, Wyatt. He's the one who got us to this level! You didn't even remember your name at the last level."

"I don't remember that!" Wyatt shot back.

"See?!" Allen snapped. "C'mon, Troy. Master G is waiting for us. We're going to learn some skills so we can get out of here."

I can not do anything. I am too slow. I do not talk good anymore. I am tired.

Chad knelt. "Hey, I know how you feel. Last level, when I was so slow, I felt like I would never make it. But I did, thanks to you."

Chad is not slow forever. My eyes are getting wetter. Hide them from everyone. I want everyone to go away.

"You all go ahead...Master G and Sensei Dennis are waiting. I'll stay here with Troy," Krista said.

Krista is holding my hand. Everything hurts inside. I want to go fast. I want to talk the right way. I do not want to be slower than everybody else anymore.

"Troy, would you come and do class? We need you," said Krista.

Shake my head no. I am not good at karate.

"Would you just come and watch?"

Shake my head no.

"Would you do for it me, so I can get my lesson?"

Krista is being mean. She is being nice, so I am supposed to be nice, too. She knows I do not want to be nice now. That is mean.

"Please, Troy?"

She is very mean... My head is nodding yes.

I am watching. This place looks just like the last one with the yellow floor, but the floor is bright green.

They are doing some kind of stuff with a big stick, swinging it around.

Monica dropped it again.

"Ha! How come I have to work while Troy just sits there?"

"Leave him alone, Wyatt. Let's just finish this," Allen said.

"No. If Troy gets to sit down, so do I!"

Wyatt dropped his stick on the ground and is stomping over to me.

"I'm not working if Wyatt is going to goof off," Allen said.

Allen put his stick down and is stomping away, too.

"I'll sit with Troy!" Monica bounced.

Chad and Krista and Sensei Dennis are still working. Master G is standing still, only his eyes are moving. His face and hands are a different color again, kind of purple. He is walking over here.

Master G is looking right at me.

"So you want to give up now?" asked Master G.

I do not know the right answer.

"You are sad because you can't move as fast as everyone else."

Nod yes.

"Martial arts isn't about being the fastest or the strongest."

I don't think Master G ever played "BLACK BELT FIGHTER."

"It's about improving yourself. Everyone can learn something from the martial arts. If you are shy, you can learn to speak up. If you are too boisterous, you can learn to be humble. If you are weak, you can learn to be strong. Krista, show them your yell. Yell from your belly! Now!"

"KIAA!"

Wow...Krista did not sound funny. She was strong.

"Wyatt, look at me. You need to set a goal when you kick. Hit this target pad."

Master G is holding the pad up high. Wyatt kicked the pad a little.

"Not strong enough. This time do not just aim at the target. Aim high, past the target."

"THUMP!"

Wow. Wyatt hit that strong.

"Always aim high. Set your goals very high. Then even if you come up a little short you will still do well."

Master G is walking over to Allen.

"Stand up, Allen. Let's see you stretch. Do a split."

Allen is sliding his legs apart. They are not going very far.

"Now stay there," said Master G.

"I have to. I'm stuck."

"Yes you are."

"What does that mean?"

"Just stay there, Allen. When ever you feel stuck just relax and breathe. Sometimes you don't get the result you want right away. Just relax and concentrate on your goal. Chad, look at me. No...look in my eyes. You're not focusing. Look right in my eyes. You miss the target because you let your eyes drift. Keep your eyes straight. Now hit this target."

"Pow!"

Chad hit it.

"Again!"

"Pow!"

"Again!"

"Pow!"

Wow. Chad didn't miss. He hit it every time.

"Monica, please pick up that staff. "

Monica is bouncing over.

"Now when you spin the staff, you must keep rhythm. You can't move the staff faster than your hand. Your hand and the stick must move together. Now move it when I snap my fingers."

"Snap! Snap! Snap!"

"That's it, Monica! You have it!"

Monica didn't drop the stick this time.

"Hey, what about me?" Allen asked.

Wow. Allen is all the way down in his split.

"Now Troy, are you ready to take class? Because there are things you can learn. Everyone can help the team."

Nod yes.

"I will watch," said Master G. "Sensei Dennis will finish class."

"Yes...I will be happy to," said Dennis.

CHAPTER 21

This is a fun class. Karate makes me remember where my arms and legs are. Sometimes I forget. Everyone is working hard now. They are trying to get better.

"SPLASH!"

What was that?

"SPLASH! SPLASH! SPLASH!"

Rain. Big Rain.

"What kind of rain is that?" screamed Allen.

"It's square," Monica said bouncing up.

Monica is right—big square water is falling on us.

"Let's run inside!" Allen yelled.

"HA! Look around, there is no inside!" laughed Wyatt.

Everybody is covering their arms over their head. There is nowhere to go that is dry.

"SPLASH!"

More big square rain.

"What do we do now?" Chad yelled.

"I don't know!" Allen said.

"SPLASH!" "SPLASH!" "SPLASH!"

"SQUEEK!" "SQUEEK!"

It's the baby dragons! They are flying around us.

"Everyone follow me!" Sensei Dennis demanded.

We are running off the green floor. The baby dragons are standing all around the green floor. They are lifting it up. There is blue light coming out. A room is under there. I see a rope.

"Okay, everyone! Get in and slide down the rope," Sensei Dennis said helping everybody in. Master G is just standing up there in the rain with a blue face. Uh oh oh! He's gone.

CHAPTER 22

"What is this place?" asked Chad.

"It's *all* the rules," said Sensei Dennis.

Papers are all over the walls...all different colors with lots and lots of words. It looks like lights are behind the papers. It is bright in here. There are a lot of big rooms next to this one. They have papers everywhere, too.

"But there are so many," Krista said and pointed at the papers.

"It would take your whole life to learn all these rules. There must be a million pages here," Allen said.

"Ha! You're wrong...only half a million. It says right here that there are five rooms, each with over one hundred thousand pages on the walls, ceilings and floors. So technically, assuming you could read a page a minute and you never stopped to eat or sleep, you could actually finish in about one year," announced Wyatt.

What if I had to go the bathroom?

"And what if you did eat and sleep?" asked Chad.

And potty!

"At least a year and a half, and most people take about two or three minutes to read a page like this. So I guess the best estimate for the average person would be about four years," Wyatt smirked.

"Sensei, why are we here?" asked Krista. "We could never do that."

I thought we just came down here to get out of the rain.

"We just have to find a way to defeat Sal, so we can get out of this level and get out of this game," said Sensei while reading the walls. "Each room is different. This room has the water rules."

Oh I see...all the papers here have water pictures on them. That room over there must be the fire room because it has lots of red and fire stuff. Another room over there has all pictures of trees and grass and dirt—the earth. In that one all the papers are all blowing around. The last room is black colors and the words on the papers looks like my glow-in-the-dark toys.

"There are seven of us. We have to all look at these rules until we find the one we need," said Sensei.

"HA! Even if all of us read just this room for twenty four hours a day, it would still take us at least ten days," laughed Wyatt.

"Just read...we might find something right away," Sensei Dennis said.

"Ha! Good luck! Count me out."

"This will never work!" Allen said.

I want to go home. Why is nobody doing anything? Everyone is just sitting. Krista just plopped on the floor

and her eyes are wet. Chad is leaning on the wall, staring at the air. Monica is sad. I do not like it when she is sad. They are all doing nothing…just like I am. Why I am doing nothing again? I am not helping. I can read some words. Stand up. Read. "U an be…"

"I'll help you read it, Troy!" Monica popped up. "You can breathe under the water here!"

Wow! I like these rules.

"That would be fun! Let's read some more, Troy!" Monica bounced.

"It really says that?" Krista asked.

"Right here!" Monica bounced.

Monica is happy again.

"Let me see. You can breathe under water here, if you hold hands with a peer."

"What's a peer?" asked Monica.

"It's like a boat dock isn't it?" Krista answered.

"Ha! No! That's P-I-E-R. Peer spelled P-E-E-R means someone who is an equal," laughed Wyatt.

"That's great, Troy! If we ever are overcome by water, we each find someone to hold hands with and we'll be safe," Monica said.

I am picking Monica.

"Look at this one!" Allen said.

Allen is looking at the floor he is lying on. "Water, water, all about. It knows the way in, and it knows the way out."

"We can use that!" Sensei shouted. "If we figure out how Sal is getting the water in, we can get out the same way."

"This is working! Everybody read!" Allen shouted.

Wow. Everybody is trying again. Good.
"SPLASH!"
Uh oh oh... Water is coming in.
"WHOOSH!" The fire room is on fire!

CHAPTER 23

"Quick! Read what you can. This place is going to implode!" Sensei Dennis yelled.

Wind is blowing from the windy room. I will read. Water is up to my knees. I think I know these words. 'THE LAST ONE TO EXIT THIS ROOM, WILL GO HOME WHEN IT GOES BOOM.'

I think this is a good rule. Point it out to Krista.

"What, Troy?"

Point! Point!

"It says—"

"BLOP!"

Mud just fell into the earth room! It hit Wyatt. He is under the mud. Sensei Dennis is running in there looking for him. He can't find him. Krista, look at the rule! She is not looking...she is looking in the mud for Wyatt.

"Chad, Allen! Help me find Wyatt!" Sensei yelled.

They are all looking....and looking...and looking...

"I got him!" Allen is pulling Wyatt up. Mud is all over Wyatt. But he is standing up.

"Ha...thanks for saving me," Wyatt said.

"No problem... Let's go!" Allen said.

"No, wait! I have to read more!" Wyatt yelled.

"We need to get out of here!" Sensei yelled.

"I can read faster than anyone! You all go. I have to finish this wall! Go!" Wyatt yelled.

"You finish this and get right out, Wyatt!" Sensei shouted back. "C'mon, everyone!"

If I stay here, I can go home. Push Wyatt out. Push! "Troy, leave me alone and get out of here! Ha! Look at this- You can become any animal in this game, just spin three times and think it's name."

Get out, Wyatt! I want to go home! Push! He is not moving.

Uh oh oh! Somebody grabbed me. "Let's go, Troy!" Sensei said. No! I want to stay.

Sensei is pulling me up the rope. Get away. He is not letting go of me. I can see the top and it is dark now. Sensei put me on the grass.

"BOOM!"

"Wyatt!" Sensei is yelling. The hole closed up and everything is shaking. Wyatt went home. Not me.

CHAPTER 24

The moon here is green and the grass is blue at night.   Everyone is just standing on the grass.

"Wyatt is stuck back at the beginning of the game. I have to go back for him," said Sensei.

NO! I have to tell him the rule. Wyatt is at home! "NO!"

"What is it, Troy?" Sensei Dennis asked.

"Ule!" Rule. I wish could say 'R.'

"What's he saying, Krista?" asked Sensei.

"What is it, Troy?" Krista asked.

"ULE!"

"Ule? Hmm...what sounds like ule? Pool?"

"No!" No.

"I can understand that," said Allen. "I got it. 'Fool.' Wyatt fooled us?"

Try a different word. Home. "OME!"

"Wyatt went home?" Chad asked.

Smile. Nod my head yes!

"Wyatt fooled us and went home! That cheater!"
Allen yelled.

No, I did not say that. I just said...wait. Did Wyatt
read that rule?

"He sold us out to save himself!" Allen yelled. "I
should have left him in the mud. Now he's home and we're
stuck here."

"You don't know that for sure, Allen," said Sensei
Dennis.

"Troy said he did!"

Uh oh oh... I do not know if Wyatt read that rule.
Everybody is looking at me. I can not say everything. Lift
my hands up in the 'I don't know' way.

"Great! I am done with this teamwork stuff.
Maybe some of the rules I read can get me out of here!"
Allen said stomping off.

Sensei is running up and standing in front of Allen.
"Get back here, Allen! We have to go over all the things
we read in that room together and get out of here!"

Allen is waving his arms and talking very loud.
"Why should I trust you?! You got us here and you can't
get us out! How do I know Chad or Krista aren't keeping
some secret rules to themselves in case they need them?
And Troy! No one can keep a secret better than him. He
can't tell you if he wants to!"

"Chad and Krista aren't keeping any secrets.
Chad, tell us what rules you read down there," Sensei said.

Chad is looking at the ground. "Nothing
important."

"Just tell us any rule you read, then."

"I remember one," said Chad. "It said, 'Follow the dragon'...but you're the dragon."

"Hmm...what about you, Krista?" Sensei Dennis asked.

"I read one that said something about water... Wait, it said, 'Go through the snow, go through the hail. You can escape at the water trail.'"

Water is coming. From there. Water is running down the hill over there. Point.

"What is it, Troy?" Krista asked.

Point.

"Water. It's coming from that hill," Krista said.

"Let's go. You all heard the rule. That's the way out," Allen said walking away.

Everyone is walking to the line of water. It is turning into something like a river.

Over the hill the water is coming out of a fountain. A big fountain. It is bigger than the top of the statue lady standing in the water who holds a candle up in the air. We went on a trip to see her one time. Look at my feet. The water here is warm on my feet. I will try that other rule I read. *'Look up at the sky. The lady will save you, she can fly.'* Okay, I am looking up at the sky. I don't see anything. Wait, a bird. No, it's a plane. No, it's Eagle Lady! Point. No one is looking. Water. Ahh. It's water coming up to my face.

"Here, Troy...hold my hand!" Monica yelled. "Then we can breathe under water."

I am holding tight. Water is over my head. Where did the eagle lady go? She can save us. Everyone is holding hands with somebody else.

Sharks! The sharks are coming. I see Sal. Air...I can breathe under here. The sharks are circling all around us. Monica is grabbing a stick off the ground. She is swinging it at the sharks with her other hand. She didn't drop it! But there are so many sharks! We have to be a different animal. I remember the rule: *'You can become any animal in this game, just spin three times and think its name.'* No one else heard the rule but Wyatt. Sharks can't eat me if I'm too big... or too little! Plankton, plankton, plankton. I'm glad it didn't make me say that. Spin Monica around with me.

WHOOSH! Everything is so big! Monica is wrapped around me. We are like little worms. The sharks are so big but they can't see me. Uh oh oh... Sal is circling Allen and Krista. C'mon, Monica. Let's swim in its eyes. "EYES!" Can she hear me? My mouth is so small.

"Good idea, Troy. Let's go," Monica replied.

It is slow swimming all the way up here. Monica is going to Sal's other eye. Poke my tail in his eye. Keep poking. He is getting mad and shaking his head very fast.

He is not trying to eat anyone. Sensei and Chad are kicking the other sharks away from Allen and Krista.

"KIAA!"

Wow! Krista scared that shark away with her yell!

"BOOM!" Chad did not miss. He hit the shark right in the nose! "BOOM!" Sensei hit another shark, but there is so much water! The sharks keep coming back. Even Sal with his humpy camel nose. Wait! Grab Monica again. Spin, and think giant camels, giant camels, giant camels. I am getting so big. Drink the water. Monica is a big camel, too. She's drinking! The water is going down.

Keep drinking, Monica! Hey, I see another camel! It's drinking, too! The water is almost gone. The sharks are just lying on the ground. I really have to pee. I wonder where the camel bathroom is?

"Troy, you did it! You stopped Sal!" Sensei is patting my leg. "Wyatt, is that you?" asked Sensei.

"Ha! I fooled you! When the cave exploded I made myself a worm and tunneled out of there. I turned into a whale and was swimming to save you when I saw the camels. I knew I had to change quick or I would drown. Ha! How did you think of becoming a camel, Troy?"

"Irsey!" I was thirsty.

"He said he was thirsty! I was too, Troy!" said Monica.

"Wait for me!" said Eagle Lady coming down from the sky.

The eagle lady is very pretty.

"You're here! That means we can all leave!" said Sensei.

Sensei looks very happy to see Eagle Lady.

"ROAR!"

The tigers are coming. Which way should we go? Everyone is looking around. Wait! What is that? The water on the ground is like a picture. It's another dragon map! I know! Chad said 'follow the dragon!' Grab Allen! Point!

"What is it, Troy?"

"OOK!" Look.

He is looking! Allen understands me!

"Everybody! Troy found the way out! Follow us!"

We are running to the head of the dragon.

"Look, a red mat!" said Krista.

Mr. G is there!

"Everyone make a circle on the mat and we can shut down the game!" said Eagle Lady.

Everyone is following her. I can catch up easy with these long legs.

"ROAR!"

More tigers. Look, the sky is opening up. It's night time out there. Krista grabbed my hoof. Sensei is holding my other hoof.

"RUMBLE." Everything is shaking. I feel funny.

"WHOOSH! WHOOSH!" Wind is blowing, and the ground is on fire. Look at the tigers…they are turning into people! Uh oh oh! I'm shrinking. Everything is turning black. BAM!!!

CHAPTER 25

It's dark.

"Troy, open your eyes!"

That is Krista's voice. Open my eyes. Oh...it's not dark. We are back. Back at the karate school. Wyatt, and Chad, and Monica, and Allen and Krista, too. I wonder if she has any more gummies?

Sensei is still holding hands with Eagle Lady. I really think he can let go now.

"Listen everyone, we're safe now. The game has been shut down."

"NO! NO it hasn't!" screamed Sal.

Sal is here. He is running at Sensei Dennis. He is trying to kick Sensei! Sensei just keeps blocking. Sal can't hit him with any punches or kicks. I think Sal is getting tired. He is going very slow. What's that? Master G is just standing next to me. Where did he come from?

"Sal! Stop!" commanded Master G.

Sal is bent over. He is just kind of dropping to the floor.

"Sal, a black belt should never go to your head. Here is your new white belt. Get up!" yelled Master G.

Sal is getting up. His head is hanging down. Master G is tying the white belt around Sal's belly.

"Much better. Here is a broom! Sweep up the mat! It's time for you to start over!"

"Yes, Sensei," said Sal.

"CREEEK."

The front door is opening. I hear rain. Lots of rain. Outside it is raining very hard.

"Troy! Krista! Sorry we're late. Aunt Nancy's car couldn't make it through the floods. Did you have a good class?" asked my Dad.

Mom is with him. She is very wet. She is smiling!

"Yes, we had a great class. Troy did so well that Sensei Dennis is going to get him a team uniform so he can practice with us. Right, Sensei?" asked Krista.

Krista is being nice to me. But she forgot somebody. Point to Allen.

"Yes, Troy. You and Allen get a uniform," said Sensei Dennis.

"YES! Thank you, Sensei!" yelled Allen. "Thanks, Troy! Oh, I'm sorry about the whole lunch table thing."

Smile at Allen.

"Ha! Me too, but not that much, because it's a good thing you did it. Otherwise Sensei would still be stuck in the game," said Wyatt.

"What game?" asked Mom.

"Oh, we were just playing a martial arts game while we were waiting," said Krista.

"It looks like Troy really liked it. I've never seen such a big smile. Have you, honey?" asked Dad.

He is looking at Mom.

"Yes, he looks like he is having a good time here. Do you want to keep taking karate, Troy?" asked Mom.

Nod yes. "O-orrow." Tomorrow.

"I speak Troy. He wants to come back tomorrow. Right, Troy?" asked Allen.

Smile. Nod yes.

"Yeah! Troy, I will come tomorrow, too!" bounced Monica.

Bigger smile.

"Alright, then we'll be back tomorrow," said Mom.

I am smiling on the inside of me, too. Karate is not like the other sports. It is better. There is no ball you have to chase around. I think it will help me talk better, too. "KIAA!"

THE END

About the Author

S. Kennedy Tosten resides in Pennsylvania and is currently working on the next book in the Troy series. The author and her husband, Dennis Tosten, head AMERIKICK Karate Studios (www.amerikick.com) and Brain and Body Builders activity centers, the leaders in helping all children reach their fullest potential.

* * * * * * *

Get Troy's Amazing Universe books wherever fine books are sold.

Or visit:

www.TroysAmazingUniverse.com

E-mail: TroysUniverse@aol.com

Printed in the United States
63523LVS00001B/328-474